THE SPIRIT MOLECULE

Ayahuasca – A Journey To Another Place

Roger Underwood

Writer's Champion

Roger Underwood

Produced by Writers' Champion
Published by MA Publishing (Penzance)
Email: mapublisher@yahoo.com
Released on November 2023

Print on Demand books are printed in each region of the continent listed and distributed there through the print on demand chain. Australia | Canada | Europe | UK | USA

ISBN-13: 978-1-915958-01-3

Cover designed by Mayar Akash
Cover artwork: Mayar Akash
Typeset in Times Roman

Paper printed on is FSC Certified, lead free, acid free, buffered paper made from wood-based pulp. Our paper meets the ISO 9706 standard for permanent paper. As such, paper will last several hundred years when stored.

Acknowledgement

I would like to thank Mayar Akash, Lowenna Helena Oft Kaute, Sue Underwood, Terry and Paula Cronick for their support.

CONTENT

When Events Lead You into the Unknown

A few years ago Tommy and his wife Sally went up to Wales, from their home in Cornwall, they were on their way to see their old friends in Cardiff. They were going to stay overnight with them so that they could have a good catch up. They spoke regularly on the phone but they haven't had a get together for a while.

At this time they were totally unaware of how eventful this weekend was going to be.   A chain of events would unfold that would end up both a tragedy and a blessing for them all.

Tommy and Teddy have been friends since school days and the same goes for their wives Pamela and Sally. This was the first time they had visited Teddy and Pamela's newly renovated farmhouse. They'd seen many photographs of their new home over the period of the renovation but this was the first time they had visited to see it since its completion. The house was stunning, a traditional stone building set in a beautiful mature garden that wrapped itself around the house. The front was colourful and welcoming with spring flowers, Daffodils and Primroses, at the back there was a greenhouse and terraces of vegetables and fruit bushes. Inside was spacious and light; Teddy and Pamela had kept as many of the original features as they were able, combining them with a modern spacious layout. They were very proud of their achievement renovating the house and rightly so, as it had taken them almost a year of hard work and a big bucket full of money to complete. For the past year Teddy and Pamela had been living in a caravan in the garden at the side of the house as the work was on going. But now the house was as good as finished and all the mess and the sounds of the cement mixers were over. They were in the house living their dream. They were excited to show Tommy and Sally around the house, everything inside had an aroma of newness about it, probably because it was! Surrounding the house they had eighteen acres of land, which they had leased out to a local farmer whose land adjoined theirs. It seemed like everything had fallen perfectly into place for them.

The next morning was Sunday, Sally and Pamela were in the kitchen cooking up a roast for their dinner, while Tommy and Teddy were sat in the living room chatting and reminiscing of days gone by. It was a stunning room beautifully decorated, the floor was laid in fantastic solid oak with a colourful Indian rug, which really set off the glow of the timber floor.

Teddy picked up the local newspaper, the South Wales Echo; it was lying on a small round oak table alongside his comfortable leather chair. As Teddy picked it up and began flicking through its' pages a small piece of paper fell out and onto the floor. It looked like some sort of advertising leaflet. Teddy began reading it.

"What's that about?" Tommy asked him.

"Listen to this Tommy, it looks like this might be interesting, the place they are talking about is not too far from here. It says there is going to be a Spiritualist meeting taking place tonight at the old Baptist chapel and get this, apparently there's going to be a guest clairvoyant speaker who is going to give a reading and her name is Eleanor Rigby!"

They looked at each other and burst out laughing, really!

"Surely that has to be a joke doesn't it? Eleanor Rigby!" Tommy replied.

Now they were both hooked, this name certainly got their attention. They were both really big fans of the Beatles and anybody else who was a fan of the Beatles would have immediately known who Eleanor Rigby was.

They were laughing so loud it brought Sally and Pamela into the room, wondering what it was they were laughing about.

"Ok" said Pamela, "what are you two finding so funny?"

Teddy handed them the flyer so they could read it for themselves.

"Where did this come from?" asked Pamela, "Eleanor Rigby, really!"

After reading the flyer she went on to tell them the chapel they were talking about in the leaflet had been closed down for many years.

"The last time I drove past the chapel all the windows and doors were boarded up and the whole building was looking pretty derelict and forlorn."

"Well I don't know about that," said Teddy, "perhaps someone has rented it just for tonight's event, and they've tidied it up a bit, I really don't know. Anyway, why don't we go there tonight and see what's going on?

You never know it might turn out to be interesting, come on let's take a vote on it. Are we up for going?"

With giggling faces they all put their hands up in the air.

"Well, that is unanimous," said Teddy, "after all it's not as if we have anything better to do, is it? We would probably only end up staying in watching the Tele."

"Yah who!" shouts Tommy

"looks like we're going to see Eleanor Rigby!" he said with a big smile on his face.

Once again everybody burst out laughing, they were all excited and intrigued at the thought of going to see what Eleanor Rigby might have to say.

None of them was particularly religious or followed any particular type of denomination that might be on offer, especially anything from the spirit world. The only reason they were going was purely for the entertainment side of it, but having said that they were all pretty open minded in the event that something could happen or something might be revealed that would make them change their minds. Well, you never know do you?

About 7.30pm they left Teddy and Pamela's beautiful home and began making their way toward the chapel on foot. It took them about twenty minutes to get there.

As they approached the chapel they could see there were lights coming from inside the building and people walking up the pathway and entering the building.

"Well, it may have been closed before, but it's certainly looks open now. I think this is going to be good!" said Tommy smiling and rubbing his hands together with anticipation and excitement. Sally and Pamela's faces were saying something else, they were looking a little nervous and apprehensive about what might lay ahead.

They slowly walked up the footpath toward the chapel until they reached the door and then tentatively walked in. Once inside they began looking around wondering where they might find a seat. A young girl who had been standing just inside the door entrance approached them.

She was around fifteen or sixteen, about five feet in height with shoulder length blonde to white hair that was parted down the middle. She was very polite and helpful and she began directing them, pointing towards some seats where they could sit, which, coincidentally seemed to be the only four seats left in the hall. It was a manky, old, four seat long sofa. Again strange, it was almost as if they had been expected.

On the end of the young girl's nose was a large Wart, it was very big and distracting. It was varying shades of pink with a texture that looked like blob of foam. It was like a homing beacon for the eyes and they were finding it difficult not to stare at it.

It struck Tommy as rather odd to see someone so young in this type of setting. With a smiley face she continued directing them through the make shift arrangement of different shaped chairs and sofas that were all fully occupied. These seats didn't smell too good, in fact, the whole place didn't smell too good!

Most of the seating was facing forward towards an old 8 x 4 table at the front of the hall. Tommy noticed four little people standing to the left of the table, they were an odd looking bunch. They were all wearing red knitted jumpers with matching red, bobble hats, each of their jumpers had a white star sewn on the front. They each had a small blue handbag with a long looped handle hanging from their left wrists, very strange. These bags were very small not much bigger than a tobacco pouch and they had a luminous glow about them. Tommy didn't have a clue what they were about or why they were carrying such handbags. Maybe they would find out later, but it was, again, very strange. They stood there looking like a row of smiley garden gnomes, all a similar height, very small!

As soon as they were sat in their seats the entrance door was slammed shut with a loud bang, loud enough to make them jump. The bolt on the door was loudly pulled across, locking the door. They were now locked in, which was slightly concerning! They gave each other a sideways glance, as if to say, 'what's going on?' Then another strange thing happened, as soon as the door was closed they all became aware of how warm it had suddenly become in the hall. It was almost like an instantaneous heat, there was no gradual warm up, as you might have expected, it just went from very chilly to very warm. This was mid February in Wales and it was pretty cold and frosty outside. But inside it was warm enough for them to take their coats off.

They sat in their seats waiting in anticipation for what was to come next.

Tommy began looking around the hall to see if he could see what could have created such warmth in such a short time. There were no radiators on the walls or any other form of heating, at least none that could be seen. It was getting very weird, with the flick of a switch it had become as warm as a summer evening! Tommy began looking around the hall at all the faces, everybody in the hall appeared to be relaxed about the door being shut and bolted. They were happily smiling and chatting amongst themselves, mainly about the things that might be revealed in the coming clairvoyance's performance. Tommy was getting the feeling that most of the people in the hall knew one another. He thought this because of the way they were interacting with each other. This in itself was ok, but he felt a lot of them seemed to be looking in their direction a little too much, because they were the newcomers there. This was making them all feel uneasy, Tommy was beginning to think there might be some sort of set up going on. Maybe, some of them were in cahoots with the clairvoyant in some way or another, or perhaps they may even be tonight's sacrifice, Ha, Ha! Tommy had always been sceptical about this type of thing, but he was prepared to go along with it and see what happened. Sally disagreed with him, saying in a low voice, "You're just being paranoid" and he was told to keep his mouth shut and be quiet! Huh! She was obviously very nervous!

Then Pamela said, in a quiet voice,

"have any of you noticed how everybody in here seems to be a little on the small side?"

"Yes" agreed Sally, "I was thinking exactly the same thing."

Teddy and Tommy began scanning around and sure enough they did seem to be the tallest people in the hall. They hadn't really noticed how everybody in the hall was so small before because they had been sitting down and their height hadn't been so obvious to them. In total there were between thirty to forty people in the hall, most looked to be middle-aged, there were few younger people there but, surprisingly of all, there didn't appear to be many older people there, as you might have expected, just by the nature of the type of event it was.

There were three people sat at the table at the front of the hall. They didn't see them enter, they just seemed to have appeared there. Perhaps the friends hadn't been paying attention, but there they were, again weird! There were two grey haired women sat at either end of the table, both with beautifully platted hair with colourful ribbons woven into them. Sat in between the two women was a thin middle-aged man with a long white goatee beard. His hair was long and as white as snow, he had it tied back into a ponytail. This made him look a little like Merlin. He was wearing a colourful psychedelic waistcoat, it seemed to change in colour as he moved, almost hypnotic. At eight 'o'clock on the button, the man at the table stood up and he began warmly welcoming everybody present to the meeting. He spoke with a calm, gentle voice. He said his name was Janna, which translated means John.

He then began reciting a prayer about the wonders of the multilayered universe that we are all part of. Tommy was surprised how interesting it was. He was a really good speaker they could have listened to him talking all evening.

When he finished speaking, he turned and looked back over his shoulder toward the four little people who were stood in the same place as before and he nodded toward them as if he was giving them a signal of some sort. Then, all at the same time, they opened up the little blue bags that were hanging from their wrists.

Janna began speaking again, saying, "Soon, it will be time for me to introduce to you our guest speaker – Eleanor Rigby. But first there is something else we need to do, and this is something some of you will remember for the rest of your lives."

They all looked towards to one other and gasped, these words gave them a shiver. What on earth could be about to happen?

Sometimes You Can't Believe What You See

What came next was something none of them were expecting. The four little people with their bags opened began to sing, it was absolutely amazing! They were singing with the voices of angels. How could anybody make sounds like this, it was almost unbelievable, the sounds they were making seemed almost impossible to create. They had no microphones or amplifiers nor were there any speakers yet they were able to produce a sound so powerful it was amazing. The sound they were making was penetrating directly into the friends' bodies, in the most beautiful of ways. It was mesmerising, they had never heard or seen anything like it before. About halfway through their song everybody else in the room joined in. At this point the sound they were all making reached a new level, it was brilliant! It was not so much what they were singing about, but more that they were making a sound with unspeakable words. It was a type of musical telepathy that transfused directly into their bodies and minds. It was a sound they could have happily listened to forever. Tommy, Sally, Teddy and Pamela were feeling like they just didn't want it to end. This was a really head tingling moment for them all, it was so different from anything they'd ever heard before! They looked toward each other, hardly believing what they were hearing. There were no instruments being used, no hidden sound systems, nothing but their voices, they were filling the hall with a wonderment of spiritual sounds that touched the soul.

The singing went on for about thirty minutes. When they had finally finished singing their song everybody looked totally exhilarated and happy. It felt like they'd all just run a very long race and all won! Everybody in the hall was looking so happy, especially Tommy, Sally, Teddy and Pamela. It was as if they'd been given a drug that left them feeling euphoric and all wanting more. The sound that had been produced so pure it was almost unearthly.

Their thought, at this moment, they were showing them much more than they could comprehend or understand. They knew they should have at least been feeling a little concerned about all these strange things that were happening, but none of them were. They just knew and felt they were safe. They had no feelings of anxiety or fear. The only feeling they were experiencing was of joy and excitement, along with the realization there was much more to this life, that, up until now, they were aware of.

This moment, and with these feelings, were triggering a memory in their minds. It was a memory, which both Tommy and Teddy shared from a long time ago. A memory of an event that was almost as euphoric as this was. This memory also involved four people singing and making music, but in a different way.

These four people were called The Beatles. Tommy and Teddy were just young lads when they saw the Fab Four, as they were called, that too was an unforgettable experience for them both. It was now the turn of the clairvoyant. The woman sitting to the left of the table stood up and began speaking, "I believe the rest of the evening will be both interesting and revealing, but it will mean much more to some than it will to others."

She went on to say that her daughter had told her there would be important things to be discovered this evening. Tommy and Teddy looked toward one another, for some reason they had thought one of the two women sat at the table would be the clairvoyant, but no, she went on to say, "Ladies and Gentlemen, please give a warm welcome, to my very special daughter, Eleanor Rigby." They were all surprised to see it was the young girl who had greeted them earlier and shown them to their seats. They weren't expecting that!

Even though Eleanor was very young she seemed to be an extremely confident young lady. She was very pretty, if you could forget about the wart on the end of her nose! She welcomed everybody to the meeting and she began explaining how she came to be a clairvoyant, telling us it was not something she had chosen, but more like something that had chosen her. She began to explain how she had been given this gift on her fifteenth birthday, adding that her mother had also been given this same gift also on her fifteenth birthday. She smiled and said, "I know some of you have been looking at the wart on my nose and have been wondering. I don't blame you for that, it's only natural you should be curious, after all it's hard to miss isn't it? Of course I would prefer it if it went away right now, but it won't, but I do know one day it will disappear." She turned back looking toward her mother and smiled. "You see my mother also had a wart on her nose just like mine, hers also appeared overnight on her fifteenth birthday, just as mine had done. For five years my mother lived with the wart on her nose, people would stare and laugh at her, they would make fun of her and tell cruel jokes about her. They would say she was a Witch and plenty of other things like that. People can be very hurtful when they choose to. This wart has occurred throughout our family history over many generations. In fact, one of our distant family members was burnt at the stake in Winchester as a Witch, she also had a wart on her nose. Luckily for Mother and me, those days are in the past, hopefully it will stay that way!" she added with a chuckle.

She began to mingle amongst the crowd, almost like a General inspecting her troops, looking at each of the faces in the room, including theirs. We were all thinking, I hope she doesn't come to me! Tommy didn't mind being an observer but he didn't want to become part of the entertainment, at the same time he felt that was exactly what was going to happen!

Slowly but surely she was making her way closer and closer toward him. Every time she got near him, he looked down at the floor to avoid making eye contact, hoping she would pass him by and talk to someone else. All of what she was saying was very interesting. She was going from one person to another and everybody she spoke to more or less in agreed with what she was saying to them. She mentioned peoples' names, it might have been about a husband or a wife, a brother or sister, aunt or uncle, and it was really spooky! Tommy noticed she glanced towards us a number of times, but then changed her mind, turned and spoke to someone else, which was a relief! So far the friends were all impressed with how accurate she was appearing to be.

Then came the moment Tommy had been dreading; she turned her gaze directly towards them. She slowly raised her arm and pointed right at Tommy and Teddy, this gave them a shudder! Then she spoke, "I have a message for you, but I will have to whisper it, this message is only for you Tommy and Teddy." How did she know our names?

At this moment they were all feeling very uneasy, everybody in the room had turned around and were focused on them. She stood by their side, she leaned in closer to them and said; "I have a message from two different people, or I believe it to be two different people. I don't have their names just their initials, the first is from somebody with the initials J.W.L. and the other is from

D.M.T. Do you know anybody with these initials, do they mean anything to you?" She stood in front of them waiting for a reply. "No, they don't mean anything to me, nothing I can recall, at least not at the moment," said Tommy.

"Me neither." added Teddy.

Eleanor leaned in toward Tommy and whispered in his ear; "I am being told you will have to use your imagination to find the answer, then it will all become clear to you. Everything you need to know you will find on the WEB. You will need to work it out for yourself, one day the answer will present itself to you and when it does I'm sure you will know it. It may take a little time but you will find the answer you're looking for. It's what you do with the answer when you find it, will you be prepared to take a step into the unknown!" She said, "Tonight, all four of you are exactly where you are meant to be. You have had the help of an unexpected friend from beyond, this friend remembers you both."

Suddenly they all became believers, but in what they wasn't sure? She stepped back and said "You're all safe now, what was meant to have been done has now been done. Bless everybody, and hopefully one day we will all meet again, sometime in the future and beyond." This event has to have been the strangest and most bizarre thing that has ever happened to any of them. They had never expected anything like this to happen!

Finally the meeting was at an end and as much as they enjoyed the whole event they were all relieved it was finally over. It had been a lot to take in.

Again Eleanor Rigby thanked them all for being there, saying, "I hope this has been of interest to you all and I hope you have gained some insight from tonight's' meeting." adding, "It is always good to have hope."

Well, they could safely say this was one of the most eye opening experiences they had ever had. It was truly mind-boggling. As she finished speaking everybody in the hall began enthusiastically clapping and applauding her and of course Tommy and Teddy joined in.

It was equal to any standing ovation they had ever seen, even though the number of people in the hall was relatively small, it was a genuine appreciation for Eleanor Rigby. Her people began leaving the building, closely followed by everyone else in the hall, including us. She stood at the entrance in exactly the same place they had first seen her. As the people passed her by, she smiled at each of them and said, "Bless you," that was all, just, "Bless you." it seemed to put a smile on everyone's face as they passed her by.

Just When You Thought It Couldn't Get Any Stranger

On their walk back home they were all unusually quiet, each of them reflecting on the events of the evening. Pamela broke the silence by saying, "I didn't like to say anything at the time in case it freaked you out, but, did any of you notice there were no lights inside the hall, and yet there was plenty of light in there?" she added, "I also noticed most of the light fittings in there didn't even have any light bulbs in them. So where was this light coming from?"

They stopped walking for a moment and stood just looking at each other in bewilderment at what Pamela had just said. "I think we need to go back and take a look," said Teddy "that can't be right. Yes, I think we need to go back there right now and take another a look."

Sally chirped up saying, "No, no, we can do that tomorrow, I think we've all had enough weirdness for one night, let's go home and recover with a nice cup of tea."

"Cup of tea! I think we are going to need something a lot stronger than a cup of tea!" replied Teddy.

They were about a quarter of the way back to Teddy and Pamela's house, when they could see in the distance what looked like a blue haze with a core of small flashing lights. It was still far off but these lights appeared close to their house and the nearer they got to it the more and more worrying it was becoming. "Whatever is going on over there, it looks very close to our house." said Teddy, with a concerned tone in his voice.

As they got nearer to the house they could see it was surrounded with police cars and fire engines. There were generators noisily running big floodlights and firemen pointing jets of water at what remained of their once beautiful home. There were many people standing around watching the unfolding scene. The perimeter of the house was surrounded by a red and white tape, cordoning it off, preventing any anybody getting too close to what remained of it.

They were all in shock and starring at the ruins in disbelief. Teddy shouted to a policeman, saying, "This is my house, what has happened?" The policeman came over to them and began explaining, there had been an explosion. "We think it was a gas explosion," he said, "The gas board have been here and turned off the gas at the mains so it's safe now." "You were very lucky you weren't in the house when this happened, you would not have survived such a blast, as you can see by the amount of damage, this was very severe explosion."

Their cars had been parked in the driveway alongside the house and both cars were wrecked. Tommy's car had caught on fire as burning debris from the explosion had landed on it. All the windows of Teddy's Range Rover had been blown out and half of the front door of the house was buried in the windscreen! The debris was everywhere, the roof of the house was scattered all around in every direction, the whole place looked like a warzone. Pamela turned to the policeman and said "What shall we do now, where shall we stay?" "Well, one thing is for sure you won't be staying here tonight, I think you had better look for some alternative accommodation for the night, and contact your insurers tomorrow. Would you like me to call anybody for you, or a taxi may be? Perhaps you should stay in a hotel for the night and come back tomorrow and see what personal possessions you can salvage." he replied.

Teddy and Pamela were in shock. Their beautiful home and most of their personal stuff had all gone. Pamela started to cry, Teddy gave her a hug and tried to comfort her, reassuring her it would be fine. Despite his efforts Teddy was unable to console her as she sobbed with despair at their loss. In the meantime Tommy got on his phone to find them somewhere to stay for the night. He managed to get them a room each at the nearby Holiday Inn and then he rang for a taxi to take them there. It didn't take long for the taxi to arrive. Sally, Pamela and Teddy got into the back and Tommy got into the front. Pamela was still sobbing, as the car moved off Teddy glanced backwards at the place that used to be their home, now all gone. The taxi driver asked Tommy what he thought had happened, saying, "I have never seen so much destruction to a house, wonder what caused it?" "The Police said they think it must have been a gas explosion. We were lucky we were out for the evening. But it is devastating for our friends who have lost their beautiful home." Tommy replied. "Wow, I'm really sorry mate." "Thanks," said Teddy while Pamela continued sobbing as she leaned into him.

After checking in to the hotel Tommy and Sally did their best to comfort Teddy and Pamela, they had lost their home and all their belongings it was hard to find something positive to say to them. They spent most of the night talking about the events of the evening, how unreal it all felt. They realized that if it was not for that little leaflet falling out the newspaper, they wouldn't have gone to chapel and they would have all probably died. To who or whatever it was that saved them they would be forever grateful.

The following morning Pamela contacted insurers and explained to them all that had happened, she was told by them not to worry about anything, they would take care of everything. They confirmed they could all stay at the hotel for as long as it was needed. They also said that if their cars were damaged and not drivable they could go to a car hire company rent some cars. Pamela and Teddy were feeling a little better now after speaking to their insurance company.

After breakfast they decided the first thing they needed to do was to go and sort out two hire cars, then the next thing to do would be to go back to their house and try and sort through whatever was left of their possessions. They arrived back at the house and in the daylight they were able to see the full extent of the damage. It was like a bomb had been dropped on the house, some of their clothes were high up in nearby trees, bits and pieces were scattered all around. The house looked so badly damaged it would probably be easier to knock down what remained, start again and build a new one from scratch. It was all really upsetting seeing everything they owned in tatters, it was difficult for them both to process exactly what had happened.

Tommy and Sally helped Teddy and Pamela to salvage as much as they could, a few framed photos, a few trinkets but most things were either burnt or blown to where ever. They agreed the next thing they would do was go back to the chapel and see if everything was as it was the night before.

They drove back to the chapel in their hire car and parked directly outside. As they walked up the footpath they could clearly see that the windows and the main doorway were all boarded up with plywood, it looked like it had been there for a long time. The surface of the plywood was covered with lichen and cobwebs indicating nothing had been touched in a long time. They stood in the entrance in front of the doorway they had walked through just the night before, yet here it was all boarded up and overgrown. There was no way they could see a way to get into the building, how could this be happening? It was sending a shiver through all of them, this was more than strange, this was super strange, it felt they truly were in some sort of twilight zone! Tommy turned to Teddy and said, "I think we need to get inside this building and see if it looks anything like it did last night." He was beginning to think they must have all shared the same four-way dream! All four of them had seen and heard exactly the same as each other, but now the chapel was looking like this, what on earth was going on? "I agree, I think we need to get inside and take a look around." said Teddy. "Let's just pull that plywood off the door entrance and take a look inside." said Tommy.

Using his penknife they began to lever and poke around the nails that were holding the ply. The edges of the plywood were quite soft due to its age and the weather over the years. It didn't take long before they were able to pull it away from the doorframe and put it down on the floor. When the ply was removed they were shocked to see there wasn't even a door there anymore. Yet this was the very same entrance they'd walked through for the meeting last night! The same door that was shut and bolted at the start of the service! They walked inside, into the main assembly hall to find it all in very poor condition, it was almost derelict. Everything that had been there the night before was gone. This was a total brain fade for them all. The chapel was totally empty and almost in complete darkness, there was nothing inside except a varying assortment of decaying junk scattered around the parquet floor.

It was now very obvious to them all nobody had been inside this building for a long time. The only thing that seemed the same was the way it smelt; it was exactly the same odour as last night! "Wait a minute," said Sally "I think I still have the leaflet in my handbag." She began rummaging through her bag, and pulled out a piece of folded paper, "Yes here it is," she said and she began to unfold the paper, but to everyone's amazement, it was totally blank, there was nothing on it at all! "Sally, are you sure that's the same piece of paper?" Tommy asked, "Look in your bag again and double check." "Yes it is, I know this is the right piece of paper, I can tell by the way I folded it, it's definitely the right piece of paper." "Wait," said Pamela, "I might have something on my phone, I filmed some of it last night. Let me see if I can find it, it was the last thing I filmed so it should be easy to find, let me take a look." She took her phone from her handbag, turned it on, pressed the play button for the last recording, but, again the same thing, there was nothing on it at all, it was totally blank! "Ok," said Teddy, "This is now turning into some sort of insanity. I'm beginning to think we should say nothing to anyone about all this weirdness. Who in their right mind would believe any of this anyway, I almost don't believe it myself!"

Later that afternoon, they decided to go back to what remained of Teddy's house and see if there was anything else they could recover. When they arrived they were surprised to see how many people were there. Some were just standing looking at what the explosion had done to the house, but there were many others collecting bits and pieces of anything they could find. They seemed to be under the supervision of two policemen who were over seeing things. Everybody had been putting whatever they'd found into large red plastic boxes. Pamela and Teddy approached one of the policemen and told him they were the owners of the property. The policeman began explaining to them that all the people there were trying to help by recovering anything that might be of value to them. "As you can see in these boxes they have been doing their best for you, trying to recover as much as they can." he explained.

Pamela looked into the boxes and both she and Sally began to cry at seeing some of the things that were in them. There was an assortment of lifetime memories in the three boxes. Teddy used to collect watches, it was his hobby and Pamela could see there were two of his watches inside one of the boxes. "Everyone has done a very good job collecting as much as they could for you. You can take the boxes with you, they are all of what's left of your home." The policeman said to Pamela. He went on to say, "Most of these people have been here for many hours, diligently searching trying to find as much as they could for you both." Pamela began crying and sobbing even more, she and Teddy were overcome by peoples' generosity, helping them recover what was left of their precious memories. Teddy said to the policeman, "How can we thank these people for all the help they have given us? They are a perfect example of the best of the human nature." "Most had originally come to see the ruins for themselves after hearing about the house explosion on the local news. When they first arrived and saw the devastation with their own eyes they were all more than happy to help out in away way they could, searching for anything that might be salvageable." The policeman told Pamela and Teddy, he said he would relay their gratitude to all the people that had helped. He went on to say "I don't think you should hang about here any longer, I can see you are all very upset. Whatever else may be found we will make sure it is taken back to your hotel for you." 'That's very kind of you, thank you again for all your help and your colleagues who were here last night." said Teddy.

Teddy and Tommy picked up two of the boxes and the policeman carried the third box. They took them to their hire car and put them in the boot. They thanked him and gave a shout out to the people who had gathered around them. They smiled and looked toward them in sympathy with their situation as they waved them off.

They drove back to the Holiday Inn in the city centre where they took the boxes out of the car and up to Teddy's room. They decided they would look through the boxes later that evening. The rest of the day was spent going from one estate agent to another trying to find a place Teddy and Pamela could rent for the next few months. Teddy's insurers had told them they could rent a property on a like for like basis and their insurance would cover all costs of the rental for as long as it was needed, so that was all good. At least now they knew they weren't going to be left homeless. After looking in dozens of estate agents finally Teddy and Pamela had a short list of two houses that looked suitable and they made arrangements to view them both the next day. One of the houses was in a place called Roath Park and the other was nearby in a place called Cyncoed. Both houses looked very nice in the photographs and both were being let fully furnished, which helped as they had lost all their furniture. Teddy and Pamela were both feeling a bit happier now.

It was about eight pm when they arrived back at the hotel after having had a nice meal at one of the city centre restaurants. Things were beginning to settle down a little in their heads, but what happened to them at the chapel still remained mystifying. Who or what had saved their lives last night? Throughout the day each of them had offered up different theories to try and explain what had taken place. Trying to make sense of it, but nothing was making any sense. The only thing that seemed to be making any sense was that they had spent the evening in a derelict chapel with a bunch of small ghosts! So far this seemed to be the best explanation they could come up with, and yes, they were aware of how crazy that sounded, but that was the best explanation they could come up with.

Their minds were beginning to settle and they were starting to think more clearly. Teddy and Pamela were ready to start looking through the boxes and see what was recovered. Teddy pulled one of the boxes into the centre of the room. Sally and Tommy looked on while Teddy and Pamela began to take out the contents. The first things to come out of the box were the two watches Pamela had seen in the box the previous day. They continued sorting through the boxes until they came to the last one, it was like the other boxes, just bits and pieces of things with no real monetary value but lots of sentimental value. They worked their way though it and eventually came to the last thing in the box, it was an envelope with scorch marks on all four corners. Pamela began opening it up, inside she came across some photographs. It was amazing that they had survived the heat of the fire.

She turned to Teddy passing him the photographs, "Have you seen these photos before, it looks like you and Tommy as young boys. Where is this, it looks like you are with the Beatles, when did this happen, who took these pictures?" "I had some of these photos as well," Tommy added, as he took them from Teddy to look at them. "My mother took these pictures back in 1964 when the Beatles were playing at the Capital cinema in Cardiff. She had two sets of these photos developed, a set for me and a set for Teddy. I probably still have mine somewhere. There was one photo of us stood at the side of the stage, one with us talking to the Beatles big security man called Mel and another photo is of us being questioned by John Lennon he was asking us how we had managed to be let onto the stage. Remember, at the time my mother was working in the Capital cinema as usherette and she was able to sneak us in so we could see the Beatles play. But it ended up very complicated." Sally turned to Tommy, "I remember you telling about the time that you and Teddy had met the Beatles but I thought you were just joking. I thought it was just a story you'd made up and it was just wishful thinking." "Yes, it really happened." Tommy replied, "We really did meet the Beatles! We only spoke with John Lennon, the other three didn't even seem to notice us." "Yes," said Pamela "I thought Teddy was making it up when he told me about it!" "No, I didn't make it up," said Teddy "we really were there, we saw the whole show from the side of the stage." "My mother took a big risk getting us inside cinema, she could have got the sack from her job if we'd been caught sneaking in." added Tommy. "So how did you get in the there? Sally asked, "Tell us how you got in." " Well normally Mother would let us in through the back door when the films were on, but on this occasion she couldn't do it, not this time, this was a Beatles concert. This concert was a really big deal back then in 1964, the Beatles were big news and there was security all around the building covering all entrances and exits, so we couldn't get in our normal way we had to find another way." Tommy explained. "I'll tell you the story from beginning to end, how we sneaked in and how we got to see the Beatles and watch them play."

The day we met The Beatles

Tommy began to tell the girls the story of the night they met the Beatles. "As I said my mother was working as an usherette at the Capital cinema in Queen Street, Cardiff. I was fourteen and Teddy had just turned fifteen. The Beatles were in town and we really needed to see them, but there was a problem - all the tickets for the concert had sold, fast. Back then in 1964, there was no Internet or the rest of the tech stuff we have now, there was no booking line or anything like that. The Beatles were a tsunami of a new type and style of music that nobody had ever seen or heard before. But we were luckier than most of the kids who were queuing up, we had a plan B. We had a contact, with my mother working in the cinema we had a very good chance of getting in there. We just needed her help. "Mother, we need to see the Beatles, can you let us in through the back door?" I asked her with a pleading tone in my voice. " No, not this time boys," said Mother. "Sorry boys, this time it's different, this is the Beatles! This is a very big event. The management have told all the staff that there will be lots of police around the building. They will be controlling both the back and the front of the cinema and there will be as many bouncers on the inside of the building as well. This is going to be a very controlled event, I don't think I will be able to help you this time boys. "

Teddy and I pleaded with her again "Mother, we need to see them, there must be a way you can get us in."

We put our heads together and Mother came up with a plan. The concert started at six thirty pm on the seventh of November 1964. There was a way we could do it!

It was nine a.m. on the morning of the concert and our plan was about to be put into action. Mother had borrowed two brown overall coats from one of the maintenance men who worked at the cinema. This man, like mother, would also let his kids in through the back door every now and again to see the latest films, so he was happy to help us with our plan. Mother had been told to be at work by nine a.m. to prepare for the concert. There would be lots of other employees arriving early, this would make it very busy at the entrance of the cinema. We arrived at the cinema steps and were ready to walk in with mother. Nervously we walked up the steps into the impressive cinema entrance. Mother was wearing her uniform; Teddy and I were wearing the brown overall coats given to us by mother's friend. We were each carrying a cardboard box. These boxes were about two feet square making it appear as if we were delivering something into the cinema. In one of the boxes mother had put some cheese and tomato sandwiches and in the other box she put in a couple of bottles of water, plus an empty water bottle for us to pee into, she knew we were going to be waiting a long while! We also took a pack of playing cards to kill a bit of time while we waited for our opportunity to slip out into the crowd later.

There was a lot of excitement in the lobby. The commissionaires were there in all their finery wearing their brightly coloured uniforms. They were like hawks observing all the different people that were arriving and leaving the building. One of them began staring over toward us looking a little a curious as to what we were doing. He called over to mother, shouting "Do you need a hand with those boxes May?" At this moment we thought we were busted, this was a heart stopping moment for us, but mother was quick, she was ready to overt the situation, she was always cool under pressure. She shouted back over to him, "No Bert we're ok, it's just some decorations for the Christmas tree. We're ok, I can deal with it."

Then, luckily for us, someone else approached him and began talking to him, distracting him from us. We took advantage of this opportunity and we continued on our way in past the box office. That was a close one we thought. We were in! We continued to make our way through various doors and down corridors until we ended up somewhere near the rear, not far away from the stage.

Mother stopped next to a door she put her key into the lock and opened door. It looked like some sort of storeroom with an assortment of different stuff inside. Toward the back of the room was a pile of spare cinema seats, at the other end of the room there were lots of boxes stacked up along the wall, there were a couple of odd doors leaning up against the boxes. There were also lots of old lampshades and different types of light fittings. "Right then boys," said Mother, "in you go, you will have to make a space for yourselves behind that pile of chairs. Get yourselves ready for a long wait before you can come back out. I'll be back later with some more food for you. I won't lock the door and I'll leave the light on for you, but remember you must stay as quiet as you can!" All we had to do now was wait it out. We began to re-arrange some of the chairs as quietly as we could and we made a little hidey-hole toward the back of them. This was really exciting stuff for us remember we were only fourteen and fifteen and this was a big deal for us. It reminded us of the times me and Teddy used to make a den in the woods. The door to the room was a double door, one side was bolted top and bottom and the other door had a handle and a keyhole lock.

For the next three hours we amused ourselves playing a game of Gin Rummy. Meanwhile outside in the corridor we could hear lots of activity, people laughing and joking, lots of banging and bumping, lots of people happily going about their business preparing for the concert and here we were hiding behind a pile of chairs in a store room!

Just then, suddenly and without warning, the door flung open and we both froze on the spot, it was a shock we weren't expecting. We almost stopped breathing for a while! In front of us stood a smartly dressed plump man wearing a dark blue suit he was with woman dressed like an usherette, just like the uniform mother wore. The man turned towards the woman and said in a whispering voice, "Quickly, come inside and I'll lock the door." She came into the room and he locked the door leaving the key the lock. She said to him, "Bill, turn the lights off, I would prefer it if it were dark."

As the man turned the key in the lock he turned the light off. We were now in total darkness. At this point we didn't really know what was going on or what to make of it. It was so dark we couldn't even see each other anymore, but it didn't take long before we found out what they were up to! There were no windows in the room the only light was a sliver of light coming in through the cracks around the door. We were breathing as quietly as we could, trying not to make any sounds at all as they were only about three feet away from us! After about thirty seconds in the darkness our eyes were slowly beginning to adjust. With the bit of light coming from the cracks around the doors, we were able to see a little more around us. But what we could see was something we didn't want to see, and it was all too close for comfort!

They didn't do much but talking, some ruffling sounds, the sound of a zip being pulled then lots of noises, lots of Ohhs and Ahhs. We felt like we needed some earplugs, we didn't want to listen to this. We had been prepared in case we were found in the room and got kicked out, but we weren't ready for this, we were frightened to move! To make things worse our eyes were beginning to adjust even more, we were able to see what they were doing, we couldn't see them clearly but we could see them clearly enough! The usherette was sat on top of the man who was lying on the floor and she was facing in our direction looking toward the chairs. I started thinking, if we can see them, will she be able to see us through the gaps in the chairs, horror! She was looking straight at us as she was bouncing up and down. I tried closing my eyes but that didn't work I could see them in my mind! We had a limited amount of sex education in school but it wasn't as realistic as this. It went on for a few minutes, but it felt like a lot longer.

Suddenly, and to our relief, the door handle began to rattle up and down, then the sound of a key rattling as if someone on the outside was trying to get a key the keyhole. Someone was trying to get into the room! Bill and the woman immediately stopped what they were doing and it all became silent in the room. She jumped up and stood over him, they were very quiet. "How did you and Teddy stay quiet with all that going on?" said Sally. "It wasn't easy, I felt like I wanted to cough, it was all I could do to hold it back, but I held it, that was defiantly not a good time to be coughing. Imagine the shock they would have had if I had coughed!" Tommy laughed. "It was a very nerve racking situation, all Teddy and I wanted to do was see the Beatles!" They all had a chuckle imagining the situation then Tommy continued with the story.

Somebody was trying to unlock the door from the outside, but this couldn't be done because Bill had left his key in the door in the inside. After about twenty seconds there was a gentle knock on the door, knock, knock, knock, then a small pause then another three knocks followed by a voice saying, "Are you two alright in there?"

It was mother, she was talking to Teddy and me, but I suppose Bill and the woman thought she was talking to them! They stayed silent with only the sound of their breathing, they waited a little while, and then the woman said, "Come on Bill, let's get out of here before she comes back!" As they were leaving we heard the woman saying to Bill, "I recognise that voice, that was May Pringle, how did she know we were in here?" "I don't know," said Bill, "perhaps she saw us coming in. You'll have to have a word with her and find out how much she knows about us." He turned the key and unlocked the door and they both left quickly and quietly.

Up until this point the only thing Teddy and I knew about sex was what we'd seen in the odd dirty mag that sometimes circulated around school. There was no porn back then, not like there is now, we knew what was happening, but it was still all very confusing, especially in the near darkness!

It wasn't long before mother was back at the room, the first thing she asked was who had locked the door and who had unlocked it. We explained to her all that we had seen and heard, mother burst out laughing, she said she knew who the two people were. The man was Bill, he was the manager of the cinema and the woman he was with was an usherette called Vera, she knew her very well. Mother was laughing as we told her what we had overseen. "Anyway boys, here are some hot dogs for you. I have to go again, it's very busy, and there are lots of things to be done before we let the hordes in. Tuck yourselves away again and wait for me to come back, it won't be too much longer to wait. Remember, stay as quiet as you can." She chuckled to herself as she closed the door.

Not long after leaving the room she was approached by Vera. She began pleading with mother not to say anything about what she might have seen or heard. Mother could see Vera was very anxious so she agreed she wouldn't say anything. As Mother and Vera stood chatting, she could see Bill looking over toward them, he wasn't looking very happy. In fact he was looking very concerned, and so he should have, as his wife worked in the ticket office at the main entrance of the cinema. She wouldn't have been too pleased to find out what Bill had been up to with Vera! Mother was a very savvy woman and she could spot an opportunity arising and she said to Vera, "I wonder if Bill could give me two backstage

V.I.P. passes for my boys, they tried to get tickets but they were too late. Do you think Bill might be able to help us?" "Leave it with me," replied Vera "I'll see what I can do."

It was about seven thirty pm and the support acts were well underway, Teddy and I were beginning to think we were going to miss the main event. Where was mother? She should have been back by now.

Eventually Vera got back to mother. As she walked toward her she had a smile on her face and she was holding something in her hand. As she approached mother, she said, "Bill's not very happy about this and he wants your assurance that these passes will buy your silence." She handed over two V.I.P. backstage passes to mother. Mother reassured Vera, "You can tell Bill he can sleep easy tonight, I won't be saying anything to anybody about this, tell him his secret is safe with me. Please thank him from me. I really appreciate his help." Mother arrived back at the storeroom; she opened the door and called to us, "It's ok boys, you can come out now, I have some good news for you both." She was standing in front of us grinning from ear to ear. "See these boys, these are two backstage passes and they are for you!" she said, waving them in front of our faces. "These are no ordinary passes, these are V.I.P. passes!" She handed one to me and one to Teddy. "Congratulations, you are going to meet the Beatles! " Isn't life strange, one minute we were hiding amongst a pile of old chairs and now we were going to meet the Beatles! "How did you manage to do this Mam?" "Don't worry about that right now, I will explain everything to you both later, for now, clip these passes onto your jackets and follow me and I will take you where you need to be. Remember, don't get in anybody's way, just stand to the side of the stage and enjoy the moment."

Teddy and I left the room with our passes on display, pinned to our brown jackets. We were entering a very busy place. We followed mother and made our way in the direction of the stage. The sound of thousands of fans was becoming louder and louder. As we neared the stage we were given the once over by the security staff, they stared down at our passes. They looked a bit mystified but they let us through onto the part of the stage where the Beatles were, it was like magic!

Suddenly we were there, in front of us were all four of the Beatles! Ringo was checking and fiddling with his drums, George Harrison was sitting on a chair playing a tune to himself on his guitar, John Lennon was busy talking to a guy who seemed to be tuning his guitar and Paul McCartney was engrossed reading something from a folder. There were a few other people on the stage, they were busy setting up amps, and testing their microphones, and then there was me and Teddy - looking like rabbits in a headlight! We must have looked very strange stood there in our brown coats. It felt like we were in a dream, we could hardly believe this was happening around us!

All the support acts had done their turns and it was soon to be the turn of the Beatles. A man approached John Lennon, he was a very large man with dark rimmed glasses. I couldn't hear what they were saying, but they were both looking in our direction. I didn't know why they were looking at us and I wasn't having a good feeling about it, we must have looked so out of place to them. The big man started walking over towards us, he was looking very serious. I thought he was about to tell us to leave. "Hello boys." he said, "I see you have some backstage passes clipped on your jackets, can I ask who you are?" "Yes," replied, "my name is Tommy and this is my best friend Teddy." "Can I ask who gave you your back stage passes?" he asked. "My mother gave them to us." I replied. "And who is your mother?" "My mother is May Pringle, she is an usherette here at the Capital." He smiled and said, "Well, my name is Mal and I take care of the security for the Beatles. The boys are about to go to their dressing room to get ready for the show, so I think you should probably go backstage now and watch from there."

As he turned to walk back he hesitated and looked back at us and said, "No, don't go anywhere, wait there for a moment." he walked back towards John Lennon who had been looking over toward us. He appeared to be explaining to John who we were.

John burst out laughing, he pointed over and gestured for us to come over and join them. We were very nervous walking over to them. "So your mother is an usherette here." said John. "Yes." I answered nervously. "Your mother must love you both very much. So how did your mother get the passes for you? Who gave them to her?" he asked. "I think she is good friends with the manager here at the cinema and I think he gave them to her." I replied. "O.K" said John with a big smile on his face. "I get it! You are two lucky boys to have the love of a mother like that. I imagine she would do almost anything for you wouldn't she?" "Yes, I suppose so." I said John made a long humming noise, and said "I would like to meet your mother, she seems to be a really loving mother to do this for you. I think I will write a song about my mother one day." It was almost as if he was thinking out aloud and not speaking to us. He paused and said, "Everybody needs the love of a mother. Ok, boys, it was nice to meet you both but you had better go backstage now." He turned toward Mal, "Can you take them backstage Mal." We had thought we were already backstage but we weren't we on the front of the main stage, with the curtain down!

We were now properly backstage. There were tables of food and drink for everyone. All the previous acts were waiting to see the Beatles play. It was fantastic! There was already a lot of screaming going on in the main hall, but when the curtain opened revealing the drums and the Mic stands, the screaming reached a new level! 'That must have been so exciting." said Pamela. "It was Tommy and I were buzzing, the stage was ready and waiting for the Beatles to walk on." said Teddy with a smile on his face as he was remembering the moment.

Tommy continued; everything was electric in the cinema and then it happened, The Beatles came bouncing out from the side of the stage. They looked fantastic all wearing their grey Beatle jackets and Cuban heeled boots. The screaming was deafening, it was continuous and unbelievably loud. They burst into their first song 'Twist and shout'. The screaming became even louder, non-stop continuous screaming! You could hardly hear what they were singing, but that didn't seem to matter, all the sounds seemed to have melted in together, it was fantastic! Just to see them performing was unbelievable, the screaming continued, it didn't even pause for a breath!

This went on for about half an hour, the energy level in the hall was incredible! People were watching from where ever they could, from the wings, through cracks in the curtain and at the side of the stage, there were people watching from any angle they could. We were so lucky to be there, this was a dream come true!

Towards the end of the show John Lennon took off his tie and threw it into the audience. They took their bows and The Beatles left the stage, but the screaming continued. The houselights came on and it was time for us to think about leaving. "Wow, what an experience." said Sally. "Yes it will stay with us forever, don't you agree Teddy?" "Sure thing, looking at these photographs has brought it all back as if it happened just the other day." said Teddy. Tommy sat looking at the photos, in particular the one with them and John Lennon. As he stared at John Lennon what the clairvoyant had said to Teddy and Tommy in the chapel started to go through his mind, "You will know it when you see it. It will present itself and you will be left in no doubt, you will know."

How crazy is that? When the time is right you will know, when you see it you will know. Yeah, that gave them lots to go on. Then, one of the pennies dropped, Tommy didn't know why he hadn't thought of it before. Then why should he have? But now he had a good idea who it may be, now he was able to put a name to the initials J.W.L. He hadn't remembered John's middle name was Winston, Tommy almost went into shock at the thought of it, but after the night they had in the chapel it seemed anything was possible. He began recalling the meeting with him all those years ago, backstage at the Capital cinema. Tommy was still sceptical, but remembering that night at the chapel, and taking everything into account it might be him, after all, the initials did match and they did have a connection with him on that night. "Teddy I've just realized one of the sets of initials the clairvoyant told us was J.W.L. that's John Lennon, his middle name was Winston." said Tommy.

"Yes, that's right, I remember now you've said it. How weird is that, I wonder what will happen next!" added Teddy.

Tommy and Teddy had always been fans of the Beatles, but they had never been obsessive about them. They had just been Beatles fans like millions of others, so what was going on? For the next few years everything that happened that night in the chapel had been driving them all crazy trying to figure it out.

Their situation felt like the film 'Encounters of the Third Kind', when people all around the world were building mud and earth mountains in their living rooms and they didn't know why they were doing it. Well, that's how it felt for them, but without the mountain! Tommy never intended to offend anyone telling this story. The alternative would have been to ignore it and for them all to just continue with their lives, which, until that point had been mainly uneventful, in other words pretty normal lives with the normal ups and downs. But after the chapel there was always the seed of something that would not leave their heads. It almost demanded they continue searching until they found an answer, it was like a type of mental torture! So here they were, still looking, it was a bit like looking for the Holy Grail.

Sometimes you don't know when a ghost is a ghost

Three years have now passed by since their chapel experience in Wales. During this time Teddy and Pamela have had their house completely re-built and are again happily settled into their new home, and it looks even better than before, if that was possible. The house is almost a direct copy of the original and if you didn't known better you wouldn't know anything had happened at all, this house has truly risen up from the ashes like a Phoenix. Sally and Tommy have not been back to Wales whilst the rebuild has been in progress but they have kept in touch by phone. Teddy and Pamela had sent them plenty of pictures during the construction work, so they've seen all the different stages of the house being rebuilt. Tommy and Sally intend to go back to Wales very soon and stay with their friends again and hopefully this time it will be less eventful! Teddy had also told Tommy the chapel had also been renovated and it was now a child day care centre for working mothers, he was looking forward to seeing the place again.

As for Tommy and Sally, they are still living on their lovely boat in beautiful Cornwall. For most of their lives they had lived around boats in one form or another both in Wales and Cornwall. When they lived in Wales they lived in a small town called Penross, which is in South Wales close to Cardiff. When they lived in Penross Tommy had been running a small angling charter boat business. He would take anglers out fishing in the Bristol Channel every weekend. This was a marvellous job and he really enjoyed it. Then one day they decided to have a weeks' holiday in Cornwall. This was forty years ago and it was a holiday that would change things for them forever. They stayed in a bed and breakfast in a beautiful fishing village called Mevagissey. On the last day of their holiday they decided to visit a town called Penlyn, this was a major commercial fishing port and Tommy was keen to have a look at all the boats that were working there. As soon as Tommy arrived at the port he knew this was the place he needed to be, he wanted to be one of the fishing boats that was coming in and out of the harbour and landing their catches at the fish market. He chatted to some of the skippers and they confirmed it was very satisfying work and if he knew his stuff about where and when to fish he could make a good living. Tommy knew if he wanted to do this type of work there would be a lot for him to learn, but he was a quick learner.

After they returned home he discussed with Sally how he felt it would be a good opportunity for them to make a new life in Cornwall. They both loved Penlyn and Penzance and he could earn a good living fishing. After talking it through they decided to do it, the first thing was to put their house up for sale. Sally would be taking care of selling the house, while Tommy prepared his boat ready to head back to Cornwall.

Within a week he was on his way, Tommy was very keen to get back to Cornwall as quickly as he could. He began his journey by crossing the Bristol Channel and following the Summerset coast, down to and along the north coast of Cornwall until he eventually reached Penlyn.

After tying the boat up in a tier of small boats in Penlyn harbour Tommy made his way to the train station to begin his journey back to Cardiff. He was on the way to pick up his car and a small twenty-foot caravan. This caravan was to be his home for the next few months. It belonged to his parents and they had agreed to let him use it until he had found a new home in Cornwall and the family could join him. Tommy spent the night with Sally and their three sons catching up on their plans. They were all very excited at what the future held for them.

Early the next morning Tommy began his journey back to Cornwall with his new home attached to the back of the car. The journey took about six hours and on his arrival he had to find a place to park the caravan as close to Penlyn harbour as possible. For the next three months Tommy lived next to a telephone box in a car park opposite the Jubilee open-air swimming pool. This telephone box turned out to be very convenient for Tommy to keep in touch with Sally, as there were no mobile phones back then. Every evening he would ring Sally and tell her how he was getting on and have a chat with their sons who were very excited about the move, especially as they were going to be so close to the beaches! Tommy paid for new parking tickets each day, one for the car and one for the caravan no one seemed to mind him staying there, so all was good.

The first thing Tommy had to do was to get some commercial fishing experience. It didn't take long before he managed to get himself a berth on a local stern trawler called the Confide. The owners' name was Dave and his deckhand was called Rootsey. This was his nickname because most of his teeth were almost gone! The teeth he had left were down to the roots, hence the name Rootsey. He was, for some reason, terrified of going to the dentist, weird, he would be prepared go out to sea in amongst the roughest of weathers with no fear at all. Tommy had seen him jump off the side of boat into the sea, totally naked with a hacksaw in his hand ready to cut off a rope that had become entangled around the propeller. He behaved totally fearlessly at sea, yet he was too scared to go to the dentist! He would never talk about it, Tommy guessed something must have happened to him in the past and he wasn't keen to experience a repeat of it.

It didn't take Sally long to sell their house, they had an offer almost immediately. There was no haggling the full asking price was agreed and the sale of their home was underway. It wasn't too long before the family joined Tommy in Cornwall. They had found somewhere to buy in Penlyn and had just been waiting for their house sale to go through. It was in a friendly terrace just off the promenade, close to the sea with a view of the harbour, perfect.

Over the following ten years, Tommy tried his hand at many different types of fishing, on many different boats, ranging from trawling, to gill netting, beam trawling, crabbing, and finally aboard the Castle Wraith a long lining boat. He decided crabbing was the type of fishing he the preferred most, so he decided to make this his job. He purchased two hundred pots from a retiring fisherman in Porthleven, his boat was now equipped and ready to start fishing. For the following ten years he spend most of his time catching Lobsters, Crayfish and Crabs.

During this time he became friendly with a guy call Jack. Jack had been coming in and out of Penlyn Harbour regularly on his boat called the Ceana Wonder, she was a thirty-two meter dive support vessel, a pretty big boat! Jack had spent most of his time working her in the Bay of Biscay cable guarding and patrolling the Trans Atlantic telephone cables, which keep the UK connected to the USA as well as many other countries.

The boats' main purpose was primarily to warn away any big trawlers from causing damage to the cables by trawling their nets over them. Jack was nearing retirement age and he asked Tommy if he would like to buy the boat from him. He was asking a very reasonable price so Tommy decided to buy it, he wasn't quite sure what he was going to do with it, but it was at such a bargain price Tommy just had to buy it! The boat was in a pretty good condition and was still in ticket, so this meant the boat could be sold on as a fully functioning working boat. Tommy set about repainting and generally tiding it up on the inside. The plan was to sell it on and make a good profit. Then he did something really dumb and suggested to Sally; "Why don't we sell our house, (which was totally free of a mortgage) and live on the boat for a while?"

Sally was not keen on the idea at first, but she did seem enthusiastic about having a lot of money in their bank account! Again they were selling their lovely home, just one street away from the promenade. It was in a lovely location and it was worth a lot more than they'd paid for it. It was a tough decision for Sally having to give up their lovely home again, but after a while she succumbed to the idea and their new adventure began.

Tommy had already sold his fishing boat a few years earlier, mainly because he was now well past his retirement age, it was time for his boat to find a new life. Tommy sold the boat to a couple of young fishermen and she left for Brighton to continue her new life fishing there.

After a few months Tommy had the Ceana Wonder ready for them to move onto, there was still a lot more work to be done, but it was good enough for them to live aboard full time. Over the following years they had made lots of alterations making it a very combatable place to live and it has been their home for the past twenty years moored in Penlyn wet dock. All the while they have been living on the boat, Sally and Tommy have never forgotten their experience at the chapel in Wales and they have never come any closer to finding a reasonable explanation for all the things that happened to them on that night. All that was about to be changed by a totally unexpected meeting with a young lady.

It was a bright sunny, Sunday morning with clear blue, cloud free sky, the perfect weather for painting the boat. Tommy liked to keep the colour scheme on his boat simple, so he painted everything white, apart from the green decks, nice and easy to paint! The radio was playing music, Tommy had a full tin of paint and a roller and he was in his element. Tommy found painting very therapeutic and relaxing, it gave him time to think and ponder over things.

He had been into the painting for about an hour or so when he looked up to see a young lady walking along the quay toward him. It was a face he had not seen for a long while, she was dressed in a bright red uniform and had a smile on her face. It was Rachel and she was looking radiant. Tommy didn't know if it was the sunshine reflecting on her skin but she was glowing, she was looking marvellous. He called out to her. "Hi Rachel, so nice to see you, come aboard, come onto the boat and sit down at the table and

I will make us a cup of tea. We can sit in the sunshine and have a catch up." Rachel made her way up the gangplank and over onto the deck of the boat. Tommy put the lid back on the tin of paint, tied the roller to a piece of string and hung it over the side of the boat so that it was hanging down into the water. This would prevent the paint on the roller drying and hardening, then it would be good to go when he was ready to start painting again. Rachel was an airline hostess for one of the major airline carriers, so she got to see a lot of the world. Tommy had known her and her bother Toby since they were young kids; they used to live in the same street as him in Penlyn.

After giving her a welcoming hug Tommy said, "Take a seat Rachel, I will be back out directly with some drinks for us and we can enjoy a nice moment in this lovely sunshine and you can tell me all about your travels." Tommy went inside the boat and made them both a tea and brought them out to the table. "So Rachel, tell me about your latest adventures, what have you been up to?" She began explaining how she had been to Brazil and had visited a city called Sao Paulo. She went on to tell Tommy about a wonderful experience she had whilst she was there. "Have you ever heard of something called the Spirit Molecule?" she asked. "No, what is that about? Tell me more." Tommy was intrigued She continued, "Well, it sort of goes like this. In the Amazon, for thousands of years the indigenous tribes have had spiritual leaders called Shaman. They are not just found in Brazil there are lots of different countries in many parts of the world that have spiritual leaders."

She went on to say, "A Shaman is a spiritual leader who provides wisdom, insight and understanding to their people. They have insight and speak of many worlds, which exist beyond the world in which we live. They believe we can all become connected to these other worlds by drinking a magical brew called Ayahuasca. They make the brew by mixing two plants together, one is the Ayahuasca vine and the other is a small shrub called Chacruna. When these two are mixed together with water you have the brew of Ayahuasca." Tommy was even more curious to know about this brew. "What happens when these two plants are mixed together, what chemical is it making? What does it do to you?" "It is makes something called D.M.T (Dimethyltryptamine) which is a very powerful hallucinogenic concoction. When you drink this magical drink it unlocks a part of the brain most humans are not even aware they have. This is why is it called the Spirit Molecule, it's also known as the Teacher Molecule or the Wisdom plant," Rachel explained.

As soon as Rachel said those three letters 'D.M.T.' it immediately sparked off of a chain of thoughts that took Tommy right back to what Eleanor Rigby had said to him on that night in the chapel in Wales. He began to think this might be the time he would find the answers to what he have been searching for. This was more than a just a coincidence, it was feeling like he was about to find all the answers he had been looking for! "So have you tried Ayahuasca?" Tommy asked. "Yes, I have and it does what its' name suggests, it really is a Spirit Molecule. You will see things that will amaze you." "Tell me more, what did you experience, what did you see, are you able to remember all you have seen?" Now Tommy was really curious. "Some of it, I know for sure it was the most beautiful place you can imagine, it's full of love and joy, a place where anything is possible. An alien world, it was full of vibrant colours. It felt to me like the place you would hope go when you die. Every soul was living in harmony, happiness and wonderment. This place was an infinite universe with so many different worlds, a place where everything was absolutely amazing. I'm so pleased I chose to have the experience." Tommy looked at Rachel's' face, she was glowing as she was recalling her experience to him. "Where can I get some of this Ayahuasca? Can I buy the ingredients to make this brew? I think I would really like to try it." Tommy asked. "Yes, you can there are lots of websites on the Internet that sell the ingredients. Basically there are two ways of making and taking D.M.T. The first way is the traditional way with the Ayahuasca brew, this is something you drink, the other way is to make D.M.T crystals and you smoke them in a pipe. It's very easy to make, it only involves three ingredients, water, a fluid called Lye and the root bark of the Mimosa Hotililis tree which you can buy in a powder a form ready to use." It sounded quite easy to make, Tommy thought, "I might give it a go and make some myself." "Are there any side effects to D.M.T?" He asked Rachel. "There are no side effects, no hangovers, nobody has ever been harmed by taking D.M.T, psychologically or physically. D.M.T will take you to a place that will astound you; you will see things that you could never have imagined before." Rachel's face lit up again as she was recalling her experience to him. The moment Rachel mentioned those three letters D.M.T. Tommy's mind went into overdrive. This had to be what he'd been searching for and now here it was, in front of him! He knew this had to be what he'd been looking for, it felt so right. They continued their conversation, but it was hard for Tommy to contain his excitement about what Rachel had just revealed to him. He couldn't resist, he had to tell her about their experience at the chapel, the explosion at Teddy's home and what happened the night they were at the Capital cinema with the Beatles. "Rachel can I tell you the events that changed mine and my friend Teddy's lives a little while ago. I will do my best to keep it as brief as I can." She smiled and simply said, "Pray begin."

Tommy began explaining to her about all the things that had happened to them that night at the chapel in Wales and told her of the two sets of initials the Clairvoyant said they needed to look out for. She implied the initials were the names of people, but it's now looking like that might not be the case. "When I heard you mention the letters D.M.T, it sent my head into a spin. Teddy and I have, been trying to find the meaning for these three letters for quite a while. So, Rachel now that you have heard the whole story, do you think we should try this DMT? Do you think it will give us the answers we've been looking for?" "I don't think you have much choice in the matter do you, from what you have told me it seems if you want answers you will have to try it!" she replied.

While they continued their chat Tommy noticed Rachel hadn't drunk any of the tea he had given her. When he asked her why she hadn't drunk any of it she said it was because she had a saw throat. Her answer seemed a bit odd to Tommy, a drink normally helps a sore throat, but he didn't want to press it.

He told Rachel how nice it had been to see her again and how fantastic it was to hear about her experiences with the Ayahuasca, he also thanked her for listening to his story. All the things she had described had certainly given him a lot to think about. As she got up to leave they gave each other a light hug and Rachel assured Tommy he would not regret it if he decided to try the D.M.T. She said she was sure it would provide the answers they were looking for. He stood watching her as she made her way off the boat, she went up and over the gangplanks and onto quay. It was then Tommy noticed something strange; Rachel was wearing red, high heeled shoes, the gangplanks were made of aluminium and are usually very noisy under foot but she managed to walk over them in silence. He thought she must have had soft rubber soles on her shoes and he didn't give it much more thought. Rachel made her way back along the quay, when she reached the end she turned back toward Tommy and gave him a wave goodbye and he waved back to her enthusiastically.

Tommy was very excited about getting in touch with Teddy in Wales and telling him all about Rachel's visit and their conversation about her experience in Brazil. He decided to ring him later that evening as he thought Teddy might be busy during the day.

Tommy was now on the trail of D.M.T world. He needed to know as much as he could. Rachel's account made it sound very simple but he was finding the prospect of making and smoking D.M.T a little bit scary. He'd never tried anything like this before and he was beginning to ask himself if he was ready to hand himself over to some alien world. To go to a place that had the ability to reveal to you who you really are, a place that will know every hair on your head. Now that was a scary thought! These little alien Elf-type people appear to have the ability to know more about you than you know about yourself, again scary. HUH!! There was a lot of information on D.M.T on YouTube, plenty of videos to study, people's testimonials, each experiencing similar things to

Rachel, so profound it would have a lasting impact on them, but in a good way.

Each of their experiences shared a common thread; each and every person that smoked D.M.T encountered little people they described as Elf like. These Elves have become known as machine Elves because of their amazing magical ability to build things and to sing things into existence. Sounds crazy doesn't it? Yes, it does! How can that be? That would be like having a mass hallucination, everyone experiencing similar hallucinations, how could that possibly happen! Well, I suppose, thought Tommy, if you are able to see and communicate with Elves from another dimension, then perhaps anything is possible! He had reached the point where he had seen all he needed to see in regard to D.M.T, the best and different ways to smoke it, it was now time to either stop or start.

Tommy told Sally about Rachel's visit and what she had told him about D.M.T. Sally was not happy about Tommy messing with it in any way at all, probably owing to his past medical history and his age, but you are as young as you feel –right? Nobody has ever been harmed by taking D.M.T, so why should it harm him? To smoke D.M.T they say you have to be in the right frame of mind, to be prepared for no resistance and to submit to whatever will be coming your way, in other words you need to go with the flow.

Tommy made a phone call to Teddy that same evening and enthusiastically began relaying to him all about his chance encounter with Rachel and the story she had told him. They were on the phone for over an hour discussing whether or not they should try this D.MT. By the end of the conversation they had both come to the conclusion - if they needed answers, they would have to try it. Teddy said he would explain everything they had talked about to Pamela, Tommy said he would do the same with Sally and if they both agreed to them trying it, well, that would be that.

After about an hour Tommy's phone rang and it was Teddy, "OK, Pamela is in agreement that we would should try it, on the understanding it doesn't include her and Sally having to try it." "Sally has said more or less the same thing to me." Tommy replied. "That's agreed then. I will source the ingredients on line and I will make up the crystals. When I've done it you and Pamela must come down to Cornwall for a visit and we will try the D.M.T. aboard the boat. How does that sound?" "Great sounds like a plan, I'll wait to hear from you." said Teddy. "I'll be in touch as soon as I've got the crystals ready." agreed Tommy. It took a few weeks before for all the ingredients turned up and it was time to start making the crystals. Tommy wasted no time and set about making them, it wasn't rocket science, in fact they were very easy to make.

There were just three ingredients needed to make the D.M.T., just as Rachel had explained to him during their conversation. The first one is Lye and it comes in a crystal form. When water is added it becomes a caustic fluid and it gets very hot, it produces a type of caustic soda. Not the type of thing you want to get on your skin or in your eyes, goggles and rubber gloves are definitely recommended. The second ingredient is something called Naphtha, this is basically a lighter fluid and the third ingredient is the root bark of a tree called Mimosa Hostililis. You can buy this either in the dried root bark form, or ground up into a powder, the only difference between the two is that one costs a lot more than the other. If Tommy chose to use the raw dried bark, he would need to buy a heavy-duty blender to munch it up until it was reduced to a powder. So he decided it was far more convenient to buy the ready ground powder.

Tommy now had all the ingredients and it was time for him to start making the D.M.T. crystals! To say he was a little frightened about what he was about to do would be an understatement, - being truthful he was nervous and was quietly bricking it!

This Is When You Know Who Your Friends Are

About a month had passed and Teddy and Pamela where on their way down to Cornwall from Wales. But the day before they were due to arrive something happened that Tommy found really very disturbing.

He needed to drive to Penlyn to pick up some anodes for his boat. As he was walking down the fish quay, ahead of him was a face he recognized, a young man was walking toward him. As he came closer Tommy could see it was Toby, Rachel's Brother. He had just got back from three days fishing at sea and he smelt very fishy so Tommy kept his greeting to a handshake. "Hi Toby, long time no see, my friend, I hope you have you been keeping well." Tommy was expecting to hear the usual type of reply, like 'yeah, I am doing fine' or something similar to that, but that didn't happen. Toby looked up at him and said, "Did you hear about Rachel's death?" Tommy went quiet, he was stunned by this news and his head was spinning, he couldn't believe what he had just heard. "Yes," he continued "she was hit by a car while she was in Brazil on holiday, about two months ago."

Tommy just stood there with his mouth open. He was thinking he must have misheard what Toby had said. Toby went on to say that Rachel's funeral had taken place in Brazil and she had been buried there, most of the family had not long got back. "It's all very sad, but we gave her a good send off." Tommy just stood there in a whirlpool of thoughts, what on earth is going on. He was trying his best to remain calm. "I'm finding it very difficult to know what to say to you Toby, please except my condolences."

Tommy was feeling very troubled by Toby's news, as you can imagine. At this moment his dilemma was whether or not he should say anything to Toby about his meeting with Rachel just the week before. He decided best not. He wished Toby well and invited him to call in and see him at the boat if he should ever need a chat about anything. Toby wished him well, they shook hands and they both continued along on their way, except now he'd forgotten why he went to the quay in the first place, he was in a complete daze. He felt like his head was going to explode with an information overload! It was as if he'd had a handful of words and sentences jumbled up in his brain, all with different scenarios. The short conversation he'd had with Toby had really disturbed him; he needed to get back to the boat and talk to Sally.

Sally could hardly believe what Tommy was telling her. She said to him, "Do you understand what this means, it means you must have had a cozy conversation with a ghost! The only reason you're both going to be trying the D.M.T. tomorrow, is because the ghost of Rachel told you to! What are going to say to Teddy and Pamela when they arrive? They will be here in a couple of hours."

"I am not sure whether I should say anything about it to Teddy, he will only worry about it." "No," said Sally, "you need to tell him, you can't, not tell him, that wouldn't be right, you have to tell him. After all if it were not for her testimony you probably wouldn't even be trying D.M.T. at all." "O.K, I'll tell them when they arrive." Tommy agreed. "Can you believe this, this is the second time I have had a conversation with a ghost and I will probably be doing it again tomorrow! I must be more tuned into ghosts than the rest of you." he laughed.

Looking back on Rachel's visit that day Tommy knew there something not quite right, even when he gave her a hug it didn't feel like a hug, it felt like he was barely touching her. Then there was this beautiful glow she had about her and the tea he made her, she didn't drink, she said she had a saw throat, that didn't make much sense. When she was leaving the boat, walking across the gangplanks she made no sound at all. Normally peoples' shoes make a lot of noise as they cross the gangplank, but she walked across like she was on air. Tommy knew something wasn't right, but he never thought she was a ghost!

The phone rang and it was Teddy, he was ringing to let them know they were about to pull onto the quay. Sally and Tommy left the boat and went down the quay to greet them. Teddy parked his Range Rover alongside the Ceana Wonder' mooring, they all gave each other lots of hugs and made their way over onto the boat. They had been friends for so long, from young to old, they were family and they had an unbreakable bond between them. If Tommy was hanging off the edge of a cliff by his finger tips he knew Teddy would be there to help pull him back up, that's how close to each other they were. Sally wasted no time cooking a fry up for them all and before they knew it they were sitting around the table as if they had never been apart. "I thought this might be a good time to bring up the topic of Rachel." Tommy said to Teddy and Pamela. "I have some news for you both which is both good and bad." "That's not sounding good Tommy." replied Teddy. Tommy began by reminding them about the original conversation that he had with Rachel. It was based on that conversation that they were going to try the D.M.T. Teddy turned to me, "OK, so what's changed with Rachel's story?" "Well," continued Tommy, "the story basically remains the same, but it's more like Rachel has changed, she was not who she appeared to be when she told me about D.M.T. There is no easy way to say this; Rachel died in a road accident in Brazil." "Oh, that's terrible." said Pamela. "Yes, it is, it is terrible but the problem we have is Rachel died two months ago, this is well before my conversation with her. I know it sounds crazy but it's true."

Tommy went on to tell them about his encounter with Rachel's brother on the fish quay, and how he told him about Rachel's death. "What are your thoughts on it?" he asked them.

"Do you think we should still go ahead and try the D.M.T., after all we did make our decision to try it based on what now turns out to be on the say so of a ghost." Teddy and Pamela answered almost in a perfect synchronization, "Wow, that is mental, that's some story Tommy." "Surly you won't be going ahead trying the D.M.T. now, will you!" said Sally. "Ok, let's for a moment not consider the bad news. Let's look at the good news. For a start, we are all still alive; if it were not for the night we spent at the chapel we wouldn't even be here to consider anything, so that's good. It seems to me these spirits have brought us this far so I think we should be trusting the ghost of Rachel, after all she has taken the time to come from another place to us and tell us what we need to be doing next. I think we should listen to her, I feel sure we need to continue and see what happens." "I agree." said Teddy "we need some answers, I think we need to do it. Something has been leading us along this road, this is something we are meant to find out."   They were all now in agreement and no matter how strange things had become they all knew there had to be a good reason for all the things that had happened to them over the years. Each of them was very aware there must be a bigger picture for them to see. The plan was for them to try the D.M.T. the following day, Saturday.

They spent most of the rest of Friday discussing their plan of action.

They decided they would smoke the D.M.T. at the same time as each other. They would sit on the settee in the living room and try and relax as much as was possible, easier said than done! On Saturday evening they decided to go out for a meal at the local Indian restaurant. "You never know, it might be our last meal here on earth!" joked Teddy. It was a very nice meal and they all enjoyed themselves, just what they needed to lighten things up and help relax them ready for their experience.

Tommy thought he might have made a bit too much of the crystal, but better to have too much than not enough. He weighed the crystal and it came to a little over three grams. By now it was late in the evening, Pamela and Sally were to be their assistants on this little adventure. They decided Teddy and Tommy would sit side by side on the edge of the settee and Pamela and Sally would kneel down in front of them in between their legs. Each of the girls held one of the glass pipes that Tommy had bought on line. The pipes had a narrow stork and at the end of it was a bubble with a small hole at the top, this was where the crystals were to be put.

Everybody was jittery and nervous about what was about to happen. The recommended amount of crystal needed was just the tip of a teaspoon, so Tommy put this amount into each of the bowls and passed them back to the girls. He gave them both a pair of white cotton gloves and a cigarette lighter each, they would need the lighter to heat up the crystals in the bowl and the gloves would protect their fingers from the heat. Tommy told them they needed to hold the stork of the pipe close to the bowl and then heat the crystals. They had to heat the crystals up at the same time as each other until the bowls were full of smoke. When they had done this they had to swivel the pipes around and place them in Tommy and Teddy's mouths. "Have you got that girls, are you ok to start?" said Tommy. "Yes, no problem we are ready. Are you two still good to go?" asked Sally. "Yes." he replied. "Teddy this is what we will do, as soon as we have inhaled the smoke into our mouths, I will slap my leg, then we can get the timing just right and we can breathe in together." "Okey dokey." replied Teddy, which was a pretty calm comment under the circumstances!

Everything was ready and they were good to go for it. The girls were ready and waiting, looking eager to put a flame under the crystals. But was Tommy ready, he sure hoped so! He told to girls to burn the crystals and make smoke. It didn't take long for the bowls to fill up; they were ready to begin their journey, God knows where too! The girls kneeled in front of them holding the pipes up to the boys open mouths. Tommy raised his hand and slapped his leg. They inhaled a good mouthful of the crystals' smoke, what happened next was totally unexpected. Both of them coughed at the same time and blew out the smoke from their mouths, directly into the open mouthed faces of Pamela and Sally! They were most defiantly were not expecting that, they were just sat there like two zombies! Sally and Pamela had never taken drugs in their lives! Now they had started, straight into the deep end! Tommy didn't quite know what to say to them, they couldn't see much of their faces as their heads were hanging down limply, but they seemed to be happy enough. Both were sat in exactly in the same position they were in when they put the pipes into their mouths. Teddy and Tommy were looking at each other and they just burst out laughing - but as quietly as they could! "Are you ok Darling?" Teddy asked Pamela. She paused for a moment and replied, " I did want to kill you, but now being wherever this is, I forgive you. This place is amazing, let me be for a little while." Tommy kneeled down on the floor alongside Sally, "You ok Sally?" "Oh my Lord, I'm definitely ok!" she replied.

Teddy and Tommy had been smokers for years, but they had both stopped smoking more than fifteen years ago. They may have thought they were ready for it but when they took such a big toke their lungs certainly weren't. But at least now they knew what to expect, "I think in the next attempt we'll be fine." Tommy reassured Teddy.

All they could do now was wait for Pamela and Sally to come back. "It's not supposed to last for more than ten minutes so they should be back with us soon." Tommy said to Teddy. It was coming up to ten minutes and they began lifting their heads and opening their eyes. Pam was first to speak, "That was amazing, I never thought I would ever see anything like that." Then Sally spoke, she had a tear running down her face, "I was feeling so over joyed by all the things I was seeing I didn't even think of Pamela." "So what is it that you saw?" asked Teddy. "I think it is impossible to explain to you, there was so much to take in, but what I can say is this place is full of love." answered Sally. "Yes," said Pamela, " that's exactly the same feeling I was getting. I was always aware that I was still here sat on the floor, but at the same time I was in this magical world somewhere else, it was like my physical body remained here and a copy of me went there! I don't know if anybody would be able to bring any memory back from this place, none of the things I've seen could be brought back." "Yes," said Sally, "it was the same for me, as I was coming back I could feel the memory of it all slowly fading away." "Were you there together, did you see each other while you were there?" asked Teddy. "No, I didn't see Pamela the whole time I was there, there was so much going on. It felt like there were miracles being created all around me, it also felt like I had been there for hours, not minuets. There is one thing that I can remember clearly, it was the sound of singing and this singing was exactly the same style of singing as we heard at the chapel back in Wales. The singing was constant and continued the entire time I was there."

Pamela agreed it was the same for her, except she was able to recall seeing a row of little people wearing red jumpers with white stars on the front, exactly the same as we saw in the chapel. "Ok, I need to see this for myself." said Tommy.

Roger Underwood

This Is When We Find Out Ayahuasca Really Works

While they'd been waiting for the girls to return from their unexpected experience, Tommy and Teddy had been busy reloading the pipes, ready to have another attempt when the girls came back. Now it was their turn, except this time Pamela and Sally insisted they wear facemasks, they said as much as they enjoyed their experience, they were not ready to do it again! They knew enough now to know there was more to this life than they could have imagined and even more about the next.

They all sat in exactly the same position as they had been the first time they tried to smoke it, except this time Sally and Pamela were more prepared. "Are you ready?" asked Pamela. "Yes, we're ready." replied Tommy and Teddy.

The girls lit up the lighters and turned them up to full. They began heating up the crystals until the bowls were full of smoke. They quickly turned the pipes around and placed the ends into Tommy and Teddy's mouths. They looked at each other and Teddy gave the signal by slapping his leg. They both inhaled the smoke into their lungs at the same time. They held in the smoke for as long as they could before exhaling it - as recommended on YouTube. Once they had exhaled the smoke Pamela and Sally knew they were now somewhere else, they would be in two different places at the same time. Pamela was first to speak saying, "Are you both ok?" "Yes, I am ok. This place is amazing." said Teddy and he began laughing out loud. Sally then asked Tommy if he was feeling happy with where he was. He said, "I'm not sure where I am, it's very dark where I am and there's lots of strange noises around me like a very deep growling sound and it's around me, I am not liking this at all, this is not a good feeling."

Sally and Pamela were very concerned with Tommy's comment but there was nothing they could do about it now, wherever he was he would have to stay there until the effect of the crystals wore off and it was time for him to come back. Teddy on the other hand, was grinning and laughing as he was having the time of his life, and he shouted out loud, "This place is just too much, it's fantastic!" and he began laughing again.

Suddenly Tommy screamed out loud, so loud it made Pamela and Sally jump away from where he was sitting. It was the loudest scream he could have made. Then he began to whimper and his face was contorted as if he was either in pain or he was seeing something else or somebody that was in pain, either way this wasn't good. Pamela and Sally were really frightened, watching what was happening to Tommy. His face had turned very pale. Tommy was obviously not experiencing the same things as Teddy. Teddy had a very happy looking face, he's hasn't stopped smiling since he went to wherever he was. Tommy was crying and had tears running down his face, he was shouting out aloud, "No, no, no!" stop, don't do that!" They just couldn't begin to imagine what he was looking at.

Sally started to panic, she didn't know what to say or do for the best. She just stood there looking into Tommy's face, very concerned about what was happening to him. They were near the ten-minute time average, when Teddy started to come back. But Tommy remained wherever he was, moaning and groaning. Teddy was also very concerned for Tommy, asking him, "Are you ok Tommy?"

"Yes," he replied "I'm ok, please wait."

They all stood around him waiting for him to come back, when suddenly he gave out a huge, loud gasp and the colour came back to back to his cheeks. He was back!

"Are you alright?" asked Sally.

"Yes, I'm fine, but I have seen the most terrible things, I never want to go back there ever again. It was the worst nightmare you could imagine, there were people in this place who were living in an eternity of fear and pain. In this place lives the biggest multi-coloured snake you can imagine. This snake was so big there was no way of knowing where it ended. Its' mouth was open and inside it was full of human eyes, coldly staring at everything that came into its' mouth. These eyes were all that remained of human souls after the snake had consumed them. The snake wanted everything that was bad and if it could take a good soul into its' mouth that would please it more. Its' head was as big as a city with huge brown fangs dripping with blood. Inside the snake was where its' children lived. These children are demons, they are the torturers of all those that entered its' belly. It seemed to me that Heaven and Hell could exist side by side, just one footstep apart. When I entered this place I knew I had taken a wrong turning, this was not where I was expecting to be. This was not what I was expecting to see, I thought I was going to wonderland, but between here and there something must have gone wrong. I think I must have been tempted by the snake in some way, because I was being pulled toward its' big mouth, or, it might have been moving toward me, either way this was a terrible place to be heading. But it was too late, I was well inside its' mouth. I was amongst millions of staring eyes, all looking at me. It felt like I was being sucked into a big black hole with all these eyes staring at me, they were twinkling like little stars. While I was in this darkness I witnessed many terrible and horrible things. I needed to get out and away from this place, it was far too distressing, I really needed to get out of there as soon as possible. Then the most amazing thing happened, I could hear the sound of singing and it was becoming louder and louder and it was sounding very familiar. I could feel the music vibrating all around me and I could feel myself being pulled back away from the snake. Suddenly I was out of its' mouth and in a split second I found myself in a totally different place, a place full of light. I was stood in front of all of the people who were at the chapel back in Wales. They were all singing from the top of their little lungs. Their singing was so amazing, it could move and create things using musically choreographed vibrations. I saw things I'm no longer able to remember or bring back and write about, but I did see many wonders while I was with them. All of these spirit people looked the same as the ones we saw in Wales, except now they were all a lot smaller, barely reaching my waist. Janna was the first to speak to me, saying, "You have seen the place you have just come from and you have seen where you are in this realm, which do you prefer?" then he smiled and said, "There is no need to answer." He continued, "Most human beings are afraid of death, but no need. Nobody has to die twice; all are welcomed into this place once you have left the flesh. In this beautiful realm, all expectations are fulfilled. The rules are simple, all you need to do to come here is do more good than you do bad, if you can do this, you will be welcomed into this realm."

Just then I noticed somebody waving at me, it was Rachel, I was so pleased to see her there. She didn't speak she just looked at me and smiled. I was so pleased to know she was safe and happy in this place. Stood alongside her was John Winston Lennon he was also waving with a satisfied smile on his face.

Next to speak to me was Eleanor Rigby, she no longer had the wart on her nose. She said to me, "You need to write your story and people will listen to what you have to say. This is the message you needed know, this is the answer everybody needs to discover, this is the answer."

She went on to say, "You could have died that night when you were all at your friends home, but you didn't because there is a story that needs to be told, and you were all part of that story. You have seen where we are and how good it is where we come from. There is enough space for everyone. We have welcomed everyone from the biggest to the smallest, from the most ferocious to the most timid. But for many others they will not be coming, they will be becoming eyes in the mouth of the snake, they will be witnessing all the new arrivals that are constantly pouring into its' mouth every second of every day. All that is needed to come to our place of light is to choose between good or bad, right or wrong, everybody has been given the choice and everybody is given the time to change. Through this story you will be able to see what needs to be seen, you've been shown many bad things for good reasons. You have been shown the badness that lay ahead on the road to riches. This road will lead you straight into the mouth of the snake, this place should be known as HELL. It is for us all to understand and to do better with ourselves. We must remember actions and consequences do matter, be loving, be kind, be generous, be helpful, be understanding, have pity on those less fortunate than yourselves, put aside greed and selfishness and when you have done this, do not expect anything in return."

Tommy was shaking as he re-called his experience to the others. Sally put her arms around his and comforted him, reassuring him, he was ok and he was back with them. "I'm glad I didn't see all those things, I don't think I would be able to shake off the memories." said Teddy.

"Me too." added Pamela.

"I don't want to think about it anymore. Luckily as I'm coming too most of the bad memories are starting to fade all that remains clear are the sounds of the singing Elves, Rachel's smiling face and the feeling of unconditional love." said Tommy.

They were all back from the wonderland of Ayahuasca, and they had re-lived their individual memories of the things they had seen and experienced. They concluded this Ayahuasca was something for each individual to experience. They had each seen many beautiful and magical things on this adventure that had appeared as real as real could be. They had all individually seen enough to know that there is much more going on in our brains than the things we interpret through our eyes.

They concluded that if everybody could share their experience the world would become a better place over night.

The four friends sat together holding hands processing their thoughts. They knew their lives would never be the same again.

369 4X

Other book by the Author

Prior to writing this adult genre book Roger had written two children's books. He has a very creative mind and imagination and is a hands on grandfather which has inspired his story telling.

In his children's books he uses local history, folklore, legends and the lives of the people who lived in West Cornwall generations before him. He brings the stories to life incorporating mystery and intrigue.

The children's books are based in Newlyn, Mousehole, Paul and the Isles of Scilly. They tell of a fishing family, their lives, faith, customs and traditions with some mystery and enchantment. The main characters are two young boys, a magic Acorn and a very special Dolphin.

Roger missed out on the Holyer an Gof award for his 1st book but his sequel got nominated for the award in 2023.

Book 1: **Smiley and the Acorn – A Story from Cornwall**

This is a story of one little acorn that grew into a magnificent, magical tree and a chain of events that followed involving three generations of one Cornish family. The mystical journey of the tree was in the hands of an ordinary, hard working fisherman and was passed down through his boatbuilding sons to his grandsons Denzil and Jago and a very special boat. The ACORN was built from the tree that grew the acorn. The ACORN takes Denzil and Jago on many adventures. Along the way they discover just how special she is. The lesson they learn show them how precious a life they have. Published: 25.2.2021

Book 2: **Smiley and the Acorn – Treasure on the Isles of Scilly**

The adventures of Denzil and Jago continue, with even more surprises. They go on a camping holiday to the Isles of Scilly, with their girlfriends Tamsyn and Nessa. As they sail across to the islands aboard their boat the Acorn, they are accompanied by their very special friend Smiley the dolphin. Their trip is full of surprises for them all except Smiley. He leads them to make a very special discovery on the seabed off Bryer Island. Their discovery answers questions about the historical mysteries of West Cornwall. It brings joy and pride to everyone when the treasure is returned to its home. Once again Smiley plays a very special part in their destiny. Published 6.6.2022

Holyer an Gof

The annual Gorsedh Kernow Holyer an Gof Awards were instigated in 1996 for books published in 1995 and are so named in memory of Redruth publisher and Cornish Bard Leonard Truran, whose Bardic name was Holyer an Gof – Follower of The Smith. The scheme was established and is organised by Bards of Gorsedh Kernow to promote books about Cornwall, set in Cornwall or in Cornish (Kernewek).

Each year about 60 – 80 books are submitted by publishers from Cornwall and beyond and these are read and evaluated by members of a panel of Readers. The winning entries are announced at a presentation evening held in July.

There are 12 categories, each nominated book receiving a Gorsedh Kernow Certificate. There is a winning book in each class/sub-class, which receives a Gorsedh Kernow Winner's Certificate.

(Source: website https://gorsedhkernow.org.uk/holyer-an-gof-publishers-awards/)